This Little Hippo
book belongs to

_____

_____

*best wishes*
*Mike Dickinson*

Scholastic Children's Books,
Commonwealth House, 1-19 New Oxford Street,
London WC1A 1NU, UK
a division of Scholastic Ltd

London • New York • Toronto • Sydney • Auckland

First published in the UK in 1997 by Little Hippo,
an imprint of Scholastic Ltd

Copyright © Mike Dickinson 1997

ISBN 0 590 19454 2

Printed and bound in Spain by G.Z. Printek

# Where Next, Mr Noah?

Mike Dickinson

Little
Hippo

Mr and Mrs Noah and all the animals had been cooped up in the Ark for weeks and weeks. They were running out of food and everyone was feeling grumpy.

One day the rain stopped and the sun came
out. Mrs Noah danced out on deck.
"It's stopped raining," she said folding up
her umbrella.

"Come along, Mr Noah," she called. "The rain has stopped and we're on dry land . . . there's a lot to do."

Mr Noah opened the huge doors of the Ark.
"Everybody out!" he yelled. "It's safe to leave
the Ark."

The animals came out slowly, two by two.
There was quite a bit of pushing and shoving,
but soon they were all on dry land.

Mr Noah waved his arms and shouted, "Off you
go then . . . Skat! Shoo! Shoo!"
"But where do we 'shoo' to?" asked the animals.

"Oh dear, oh dear," said Mr Noah. "Do I have to do everything?"

He stomped back into the Ark and pulled an atlas down from the bookshelf.

He opened it at page one.

"Africa," read Mr Noah out loud, "is big and
hot with plenty of trees. Now . . . who wants to
go to Africa?"

Lots of animals wanted to go to Africa. They lined up and Mr Noah wrote their names down.

Finally, he said, "That's enough now . . . Africa is full."

The kangaroos were next in line. They wanted to go to Africa. They jumped up and down and begged Mr Noah to let them go too.

"Australia is the place for you," he said. "There's plenty of room for jumping."

It took a long time to find homes for all the animals. When Mr Noah turned to the last page of the atlas, all the animals knew where they were going. Well, nearly all of them did . . .

The rats couldn't wait and ran off without telling anyone where they were going.

"Oh dear," said Mrs Noah. "They could be anywhere by now."

And the fleas were so fond of the dogs that they didn't want to leave them.

"We'll go where the dogs go," said the fleas.

"Ahhh!" said Mr Noah. "Isn't that nice."

The boa constrictors wanted to play with Mr Noah, but he didn't think it was much fun. He quickly found them somewhere to go.

The pandas were still feeling seasick.
"Bamboo shoots are good for wobbly tummies,"
said Mr Noah and he wrote their names down
for China.

The elephants couldn't decide whether to go to Africa or India. Mr Noah closed his eyes, spun round three times and said, "Big ears go to Africa, little ears go to India."

As for the camels, they were being very fussy. They looked down their noses at the atlas and wouldn't choose.

"Stay here, for all I care," said Mr Noah.

The gorillas thought the seaside would be exciting, but Mr Noah said, "Climbing trees is much more fun. We'll find you a forest."

The huge condors said they wanted to go to a nearby country so they didn't have to fly very far.

"Lazy birds," said Mr Noah as he looked at the condors' wide wings. He sent them off to South America, on the other side of the world.

At last the animals were ready to leave.

Mrs Noah drew them all a map and Mr Noah
tied labels round the little ones so they wouldn't
get lost.

Mrs Noah made a speech and Mr Noah gave
every animal a packed lunch to eat on the way.

As Mr Noah waved goodbye to the last animal, Mrs Noah went inside to make a cup of tea.

"Goodness me!" she cried. "Come and look at this!"

Look at the mess those animals have left," she gasped. "We can't sit down till we've cleaned this ark from top to bottom."

Mrs Noah opened all the windows and dusted in all the corners. Mr Noah swept the floors and looked under all the beds.

At the bottom of the Ark he found a pair of penguins, fast asleep.

"Oh dear," said Mr Noah. "Everyone else has gone, but don't cry. We'll find you somewhere to go."

Mr and Mrs Noah looked through the atlas, and checked the list. At last Mr Noah said, "There's plenty of room at the South Pole. It's a bit cold, but the scenery is splendid."

Mr Noah looked round the empty Ark. He felt sad now all the animals had gone. Mrs Noah gave him a hug.

"Never mind, dear," she said. "There's just one more thing . . . "

"Oh no," said Mr Noah. "I've had enough. If
there are any more animals left . . . they will
just have to stay with us."

"I was hoping you would say that," said Mrs
Noah happily.